W9-ARZ-767

RECEIVED
OHIO DOMINICAN
COLLEGE LIBRARY
COLUMBUS, OHIO
43219

Muriel Stanek

Growl When You Say R

Pictures by Phil Smith

Albert Whitman & Company, Chicago

To Anna and Chris

Library of Congress Cataloging in Publication Data

Stanek, Muriel Novella, 1915-
  Growl when you say R.

  (A Concept book)
  SUMMARY: Robbie overcomes his speech problem with
the help of a skillful teacher, hard work, and the
discovery that he is not alone.
  [1. Speech—Disorders—Fiction] I. Smith, Phil.
II. Title.
PZ7.S78637Gr   [E]   79-171
ISBN 0-8075-3074-3

About this story

If a child's speech is impaired in some way, important messages may be misunderstood, ignored, or ridiculed. Even a minor speech problem can become the source of much frustration and unhappiness, especially for a young child who does not have the perspective to realize his speech may improve.

In this story, Robbie's speech calls attention to itself, making Robbie uncomfortable and interfering with the communication of his ideas and feelings. An articulation disorder such as Robbie's is the most frequent type of speech disorder. Robbie's treatment is representative of treatment for other types of disorders as well—stuttering, language delay, or cleft palate speech. Therapists and speech students will appreciate the importance of motivation and practice and will recognize the progress made when Robbie carries over a "new" sound into his everyday speech.

It is important for children and parents to understand the feelings that accompany a speech problem and to realize that treatment is available. Speech-language therapists, trained to deal with a variety of communication problems, work privately as well as through schools and clinics. Through legislation, speech treatment is now available to children of all ages in many states.

Children who have their own speech problems will be pleased and encouraged by Robbie's success. Parents, teachers, and other boys and girls reading this book will gain understanding of persons with speech disorders and may find it easier to give helpful support.

Readers who seek information about speech and language problems may wish to write to: The American Speech-Language and Hearing Association, 10801 Rockville Pike, Rockville, Maryland 20852.

Sandra L. Lindaman, M.A., C.C.C.-SP
Speech-Language Pathologist

When Robbie's family moved to a new town, Robbie had to go to another school.

Robbie's new teacher was Mrs. Rose. "What's your name?" she asked Robbie on his first day.

"My name is Wobbie," Robbie said.

"Louder, please," said Mrs. Rose.

"MY NAME IS WOBBIE," said Robbie loudly.

A boy in the front of the room laughed. Robbie sat down quickly and pretended to look for his pencil on the floor. He hardly heard what Mrs. Rose said after that, he felt so bad. What was wrong with the way he said his name?

Robbie was glad when it was time for recess. He followed the other children outside. Everybody took turns racing to the fence and back again. Soon all the kids were screaming for a boy named Harry to win.

"Run, Harry, run!" they yelled.

"Wun, Hawwy, wun!" yelled Robbie.

"You talk funny," said a boy named Steve.

"No, I don't," Robbie said. He was getting mad. No one had ever said he talked funny before.

In class when it was Robbie's turn to count, he pointed to the pictures and said, "Twee wobbins and twee wabbits." The girl next to him giggled.

I don't like her, and I don't like this school, Robbie thought. I won't ever come back here again.

The next morning Robbie said, "I'm too sick to go to school, Mom."

His mother took his temperature and looked at his throat. "You seem okay to me," she said. "You'll feel better when you get some fresh air."

Robbie went to school, even though his stomach still felt upset. But he didn't say a word all morning.

"Are you all right?" Mrs. Rose asked.

Robbie nodded, but he looked down at the floor and didn't say anything. He stayed inside at recess so he wouldn't have to talk to anyone.

After school Steve began waving his red jacket in Robbie's face. "What color is my jacket, Robbie? Say 'wed'! Say 'wed'!"

Robbie was angry. He clenched his fists. "Cweep," he said.

"Fight, fight!" yelled one of the big kids. A crowd gathered around.

"Give it to him, Robbie," yelled Harry.

The two boys got closer and closer. Suddenly Robbie grabbed Steve's red jacket and threw it high up in a tree.

Steve was so mad he kicked the tree. "I'm telling Mrs. Rose," he said to Robbie. "You'll get in trouble."

A big kid yelled at Steve. "You turkey. You tattle-tale turkey!"

Robbie turned and ran home as fast as he could. "I don't care if I'm in trouble," he thought. But he felt terrible, and he wasn't even hungry at dinner.

"Are you okay?" his mother asked.

Robbie nodded and swished his fork around in his mashed potatoes. He wanted to tell his mom and dad how awful school was, but he just couldn't.

Right after dinner, the phone rang.

"Hello, Mrs. Rose," Robbie heard his mother say.

Oh, oh, Robbie thought. Was Mrs. Rose going to tell his mother about the fight?

But when Robbie's mother hung up the phone, she didn't scold him at all. Instead, she said, "Your teacher told me you'll be starting a speech class tomorrow."

"Why?" asked Robbie.

"We think a speech class will help you do better in school. Would you like to talk about school?"

"Nope," Robbie said. He didn't want to talk about his problem, even to his mother. But he wondered about the speech class. Would he have to talk a lot? Would the other kids laugh at him?

The next morning at nine o'clock three big girls came to the door of Robbie's class. Some children went with one of the girls to a special reading class. Two Spanish kids went to a class to learn more English.

"Can I go to a special class, too?" asked Steve.

"Not this time," Mrs. Rose said.

Robbie followed one of the girls down the hall to Mr. Hasting's speech class. Mr. Hasting's room was filled with picture books, games, and puppets. Robbie saw some earphones like the ones airplane pilots wear. It might be fun to try those on, he thought.

"You boys and girls will be working on R sounds," said Mr. Hasting. "I'm going to help you say words with R's in them, like *red* and *robin*. I think we'll have a good time." He smiled and winked at Robbie.

The girl next to Robbie was wearing a T-shirt with the name *Barbara* written on it.

"My name is Baba," she whispered to Robbie. "What's youws?"

"My name is Wobbie," Robbie answered. He thought Barbara seemed nice.

At first the children listened with their eyes closed while Mr. Hasting said R words.

"*Rug, rain, red, rake,*" he said slowly and clearly. "Now it's your turn to say the same words into the microphone. Then we'll listen to the tape recorder so you can hear yourselves."

Robbie pretended he was an announcer on TV. "This is neat," he said to Barbara.

When the children were finished, Mr. Hasting played the tape back.

"That's not me," laughed Robbie.

"Yes, it is," said Barbara.

"No fooling?" asked Robbie. He was surprised. He didn't think his voice sounded like that.

Robbie went to speech class every day. He liked talking into the microphone. The children made lots of tapes and listened to many records. After a while their R sounds were more like Mr. Hasting's.

Mr. Hasting showed the children how to use a mirror to watch their mouths.

Sometimes they pretended to be fire engines. They said "R-r-r-r-r" softly at first, as if they were sirens starting slowly. Then they said "R-R-R-R-R-R" louder and louder, pretending to be fire engines getting louder.

Sometimes they wore tiger masks and ran around the room growling "Grr-rr-rr! Grr-rr-rr!" They used puppets called Rooster and Rusty to help tell stories.

"Your R sounds are growing stronger and better," Mr. Hasting told Robbie.

Robbie could hardly wait to go to his speech class every day. He even got to school early in the morning to help Mr. Hasting set up the puppet stage. Best of all, he liked to talk to Mr. Hasting when no one else was around.

Robbie worked on R sounds at home, too. His mother and father listened every night. Over and over Robbie said, "*Ride, rose, rabbit, Robbie, run, rat.*"

One night Robbie's dad asked, "Have you had any trouble with Steve, lately?"

Robbie was surprised his father knew about the fight with Steve. Mrs. Rose must have told his parents about it.

"Nope," Robbie said. "Steve likes me now. He even wants to go to my speech class to use the tape recorder."

Robbie's dad laughed.

The children helped one another in speech class. When Barbara looked out the window at the rain, she said, "Wain, wain, go away."

Robbie reminded her, "R-r-rain, rr-rr-rr!"

Barbara said *rain* over and over again until she got it right.

"Good for you," said Mr. Hasting.

"I think I said it ten million times," Barbara whispered to Robbie.

"No," Robbie teased, "only one million."

Sometimes the children played the Ladder game. Each child had a toy fire fighter and a little ladder leaning against a playhouse. When someone said an R word right, the fire fighter moved one step up the ladder. The player whose fire fighter reached the top first was the winner.

Everyone wanted to win the Ladder game. One day Barbara shouted, "I won, I won!" The other children clapped because Barbara had never won before.

In a few months the boys and girls began working on the R sounds that come in the middle and at the end of words. They practiced *carrot* and *squirrel* for middle R sounds. They said *chair* and *bear* for R sounds at the end of words. Now Robbie and Barbara could say their names more clearly. They could say lots of other R words, too.

Robbie liked to talk in speech class. But he didn't like to say much in Mrs. Rose's room. One day in reading class, Mrs. Rose asked, "Where does the giant live?"

Robbie was a good reader. He knew the answer to Mrs. Rose's question, but he was afraid to talk in front of the other kids. Suddenly he had an idea. He took his puppet, Rusty, and made the puppet say, "The giant lives on the mountain."

"That's right," Mrs. Rose said.

"May I use the puppet?" Steve begged.

"Me, too?" asked Harry.

Everyone wanted a turn. Robbie passed the puppet around the class.

After that Robbie often used the puppet to talk to Mrs. Rose. Some of the other children in the room used the puppet, too.

When spring came, Mrs. Rose said the class was going to have a treat because all the children had worked so hard. They were going to visit the city zoo.

On the day of the trip everyone carried a sack lunch. The class rode to the zoo on a special bus. The bus had a sign on it that said, "Roberts School, Bus Number 9." Robbie read the sign as he got off the bus.

There were many animals to see at the zoo. Barbara like the baby animals best. But Robbie liked the big roaring tigers. "Grr-rr-rrr!" growled the tigers.

"Grr-rr-rrr!" Robbie growled right back at them.

"Let's see the monkeys," Robbie said to Barbara and Steve. "Then let's watch the seals getting fed." Robbie loved the zoo. He was so happy and excited that he talked to everyone, even the monkeys and seals.

After lunch it was time to leave. But Robbie and Barbara and Steve wanted one more look at the tigers. They didn't see the class walking with Mrs. Rose toward the school bus.

After Robbie and Steve and Barbara had looked at the lions and tigers, they started back to where the buses were. There were many buses, but not one marked "Roberts School."

"Where is everybody?" Steve shouted.

"I think we're lost." Barbara looked worried.

"Look," Robbie said, pointing to a sign that said "Lost and Found." A man was sitting in a booth below the sign.

"Are you lost?" asked the man.

The children nodded.

The man had a microphone. "Here," he said. "Call out the name of your school and the bus number."

He handed the microphone to Barbara, but she shook her head. Then he handed the microphone to Steve.

All Steve said was, "I . . . I . . . I can't. But Robbie can. Robbie knows how to talk with a microphone."

The man gave the microphone to Robbie.

The microphone looked like the one Robbie had used in speech class. Robbie remembered the growling sounds of the tigers as he spoke.

"R-r-roberts School, Bus Number-r-r-r 9. Wait for-r-r us!"

Robbie's loud, clear words sounded all over the zoo.

In a minute Mrs. Rose was at the Lost and Found booth.

"I'm so glad to find you," she said to Robbie and Steve and Barbara. "Who talked over the loud-speaker?"

"Robbie did," Steve said. "He sure knows how to use a microphone!"

Mrs. Rose gave Robbie a pat on the shoulder. "I'm proud of you," she said.

"Thanks, Mrs. Rose," said Robbie.

Then Robbie and his teacher smiled, because Robbie had said Mrs. Rose's name for the first time.

About the author and artist

As the principal of a Chicago elementary school, MURIEL STANEK knows children and their learning problems. She's found that learning difficulties often lead to emotional troubles, and she believes that parents and teachers provide important emotional support by helping children succeed with their schoolwork.

Muriel Stanek was born and raised in Chicago, and she received her professional training at the University of Chicago. She began to write as a teacher, eventually authoring textbooks as well as fiction. Her books for young children include *One, Two, Three for Fun*, a lively counting story; *Left, Right, Left, Right!* a book that helps children learn directions; *New in the City*, about an Appalachian boy who must learn to cope with city living; and *I Won't Go Without a Father*, the story of a child adjusting to a one-parent home.

PHIL SMITH was born in San Francisco and grew up in the bay area. He has illustrated textbooks and picture books and considers children his favorite people. Mr. Smith also enjoys films, animals, salt water taffy, and bike riding.

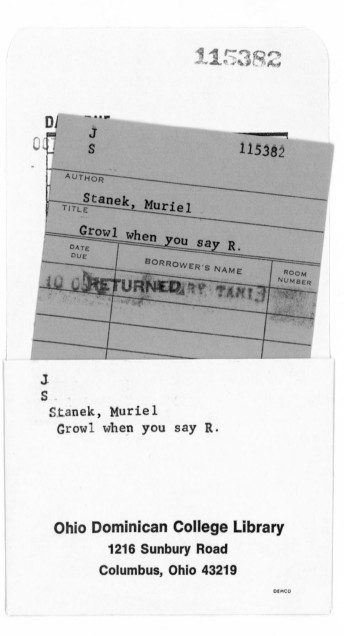

115382

J
S   115382

AUTHOR
    Stanek, Muriel
TITLE
    Growl when you say R.

DATE DUE	BORROWER'S NAME	ROOM NUMBER
RETURNED		

J
S
 Stanek, Muriel
 Growl when you say R.

Ohio Dominican College Library
1216 Sunbury Road
Columbus, Ohio 43219

DEMCO